WHISPERS OF TRANSFORMATION

WHISPERS OF TRANSFORMATION

By: Onesimus "The Blender" Malatji

Accuracy Disclaimer: While every effort has been made to ensure the accuracy of the information presented in this book, the author and publisher cannot be held responsible for any errors, omissions, or inaccuracies.

Fair Use Notice:

This book may contain copyrighted material used for educational and illustrative purposes. Such material is used under the "fair use" provisions of copyright law.

Third-Party Content:

This book may reference or include content from third-party sources. The author and publisher do not endorse or take responsibility for the accuracy or content of such third-party material.

Endorsements:

Any endorsement, testimonial, or representation contained in this book reflects the author's personal views and opinions. It does not imply an endorsement by any third party.
Results Disclaimer: The success stories and examples mentioned in this book are not guarantees of individual success. Actual results may vary based on various factors, including effort and circumstances.

Results Disclaimer:

The success stories and examples mentioned in this book are not guarantees of individual success. Actual results may vary based on various factors, including effort and circumstances.
No Guarantee of Outcome: The strategies, techniques, and advice provided in this book are based on the author's experiences and research. However, there is no guarantee that following these strategies will lead to a specific outcome or result.

Fair Use Notice:

This book may contain copyrighted material used for educational and illustrative purposes. Such material is used under the "fair use" provisions of copyright law.

DEDICATION

Being one of the difficulties in my family, always stubborn, I thank God I turned out alright. I dedicate this book to my mother, Esther Malatji. I will always love you. You have raised me well until I became a fully grown man. Thank you for your prayers and support during my tough times in life. Additionally, I extend my heartfelt dedication to my beautiful wife, the partner of my life, Petunia. You have been there for me and our family, and you are truly one in a million – the best motivator. I thank God for having you as my spouse, partner, and my inspiration; you are one of my most special and wonderful gifts. During times of trials, you have never walked out on us. Thank you. I love you so much.

I also send this dedication to my brother Edward "Gong," one of the greatest creative businesspersons alive. Thank you for being a wonderful brother and supporting me in times of need and trial. May God bless you and increase your business anointing. I love you so much. Special greetings to my sister Bertha, your passion for food will undoubtedly touch the world. I love you.

Furthermore, I extend my love and dedication to my brother Mohau; I will always cherish you, brother. Special Dedication for Galetsang & Dineo I will always love you no matter what. This is also for my friends, and fellow soldiers in war: Zama, Panana, Fina, Tshwane, Blessing, Lowen Neo, I love you guys – you are my family. Special Gratitude to my inspirer my mother. I deeply respect the gift that God has put in you, and I am immensely grateful for having you while I was putting this book together.

Thank you, my dear mother, Esther Malatji. I love you so much

ACKNOWLEDGMENTS

I extend my deepest gratitude to everyone who has been a part of this incredible journey, both seen and unseen. Your support, encouragement, and unwavering belief in me have been the driving force behind the creation of this book.

To my family, for standing by me through thick and thin, for believing in my dreams, and for being a constant source of inspiration – your love and encouragement have been my guiding light. To my friends, mentors, and colleagues, your valuable insights and feedback have shaped the ideas within these pages. Your willingness to share your wisdom and experiences has enriched this work beyond measure.

To all those who have supported me on my path, whether through a kind word, a helping hand, or a moment of shared understanding, thank you. Your presence in my life has made all the difference. To the countless individuals who have faced challenges and setbacks, yet continued to strive for greatness, your stories have fueled the inspiration behind these words. May you find solace and encouragement within these pages.

And finally, to the readers who have embarked on this journey with me, thank you for allowing me to share my thoughts and experiences. It is my hope that this book serves as a beacon of hope, a source of guidance, and a reminder that fulfillment can be found in every step of life's intricate tapestry.

With heartfelt appreciation,

Onesimus "The Blender" Malatji

6

WHISPERS OF TRANSFORMATION

TABLE OF CONTENT	PAGE

8

WHISPERS OF TRANSFORMATION

PART 1
UNVEILING SHADOWS

TANGLED BEGINNINGS

Lorraine gazed out of the window, her thoughts a tumultuous storm mirroring the raindrops streaking down the glass. Her once-stable world had crumbled in the wake of a revelation that cut deeper than any knife. Her husband, David, whose smile used to light up her days, had been leading a double life, one woven with deceit.

Across town, Patience stirred her coffee absentmindedly, her eyes fixed on her phone screen. A photo of a child's innocent smile stared back at her, a poignant reminder of the secrets she held over David. Patience's mind churned with a mix of emotions – resentment, guilt, and a hunger for the life she felt she deserved.

Charmaine sauntered through a vibrant nightlife scene, her laughter ringing out above the music. Men's eyes followed her as she moved, unaware of the emptiness that gnawed at her heart. Behind her façade of confidence lay a history of scars and choices she longed to escape.

Mishack clenched his fists, his knuckles white with the effort. The memories of his own childhood trauma resurfaced, igniting a rage that he struggled to contain. His relationship with Charmaine had turned into a mirror reflecting the abuse he had witnessed as a child.

And then there was Matilda, a puppeteer in the shadows. Her calculated moves were like threads pulled deftly, manipulating the lives of those around her. Yet, even as she orchestrated the lives of others, a darkness within her hinted at her own past scars.

In this tapestry of intertwined lives, the challenges they faced were both shared and uniquely their own. Betrayal, trauma, manipulation – these threads wound through their stories, connecting them in unexpected ways. The tone was one of tension, uncertainty, and the fragile hope that change was possible.

As the rain continued to pour outside, the destinies of Lorraine, Patience, Charmaine, Mishack, David, and Matilda began to converge in ways they could never have foreseen. The tangled beginnings of their journey were marked by a promise of transformation, a whisper that change was on the horizon – if they dared to confront their pasts and find strength in each other.

SECRETS AND DECEIT

The morning sun filtered through the curtains as Matilda sat in her well-appointed living room, her elegant exterior belying the chaos she reveled in creating. With a calculated smile, she typed out messages on her phone, each one a carefully constructed thread in the intricate web of manipulation she was weaving.

Across town, Lorraine took a sip of her tea, her mind still reeling from the shock of discovering David's affair. She watched him across the table, his expression a mask of innocence. Unbeknownst to her, Matilda's manipulative tendrils were already tightening around him, pulling him further away from the truth.

Patience sat in her dimly lit apartment; her eyes fixed on the phone in her hand. A sinister smile curled her lips as she sent another message to David, using their shared past to keep him ensnared in her web. She reveled in her newfound power, relishing the way it shifted the balance of control.

Meanwhile, Charmaine danced the night away in a crowded club, oblivious to the fact that she was also dancing to Matilda's tune. Unbeknownst to her, Matilda had strategically orchestrated encounters between her and the men in her life, stoking jealousy and fueling a growing sense of insecurity.

Mishack, his fists still clenching and unclenching, grappled with his inner demons. He had become a pawn in Matilda's game without even realizing it, manipulated into an abusive relationship with Charmaine through a cunning combination of lies and emotional triggers.

As the characters' lives unfolded, Matilda's deception remained shrouded in darkness. Their initial unawareness of her schemes left them vulnerable, their trust in each other tested by the threads she wove. The tone was one of mounting tension, as the characters unknowingly moved closer to a collision course set by Matilda's machinations.

Little did they know that their lives were about to be irrevocably changed by the truth they had yet to uncover, and that the master puppeteer's hold on their destinies was far from over.

BROKEN VOWS

The morning sunlight filtered through the bedroom curtains, casting a warm glow on Lorraine's face as she watched David sleep. Her heart fluttered with a mix of tenderness and nostalgia. It was in these quiet moments that their love seemed unbreakable, a bond forged through years of shared dreams and struggles.

Yet, as she reached for his phone to set an alarm, a message notification caught her eye. Her fingers trembled slightly as she unlocked the device, a sinking feeling gnawing at her gut. What she discovered in those messages shattered the illusion of their perfect life together.

Lorraine's breath caught as she read the words that laid bare David's affair. Her pulse raced, and a torrent of emotions overwhelmed her. Hurt, anger, and disbelief intertwined, creating a storm within her that threatened to engulf everything she knew.

She stared at David's sleeping form, a lump forming in her throat. Her heart ached with a sense of betrayal that went beyond the affair itself. It was the betrayal of their shared dreams; of the promises they had made to each other. The realization hit her like a tidal wave – their vows had been broken, and the foundation of their relationship had crumbled.

As David stirred awake, Lorraine's tears spilled over, betraying her emotions. He looked at her with concern, unaware that his secret had been laid bare. In that moment, Lorraine's emotional journey began. She grappled with the overwhelming pain of betrayal, questioning her worth and the reality she thought she knew.

The chapter delved into Lorraine's emotional turmoil, setting the stage for her journey of self-discovery and transformation. The tone was one of raw vulnerability and heartache, as Lorraine navigated the labyrinth of emotions that came with the shattered trust. The chapter hinted at the challenges she would face and the strength she would need to find within herself to navigate the tumultuous path ahead.

PAST ECHOES

The dim light of evening cast long shadows across the room, where each character found themselves lost in their thoughts, their pasts like ghosts that refused to fade away.

Lorraine sat alone in her study, surrounded by framed photos that told the story of her life. As she traced her fingers over the images, memories of her childhood danced before her eyes. She had grown up in a home marked by broken promises, a past that had left her craving stability and authenticity in her relationships.

Patience sat by her window, the rain outside a backdrop to her introspection. Her mind wandered back to a time when she was a carefree girl, a time before the world had taught her that power came from control. The scars of her own past betrayal had shaped her into the manipulator she had become.

Charmaine stared at her reflection in the mirror, her eyes haunted by a history of abuse that she had hidden beneath layers of bravado. Each man she had let into her life had left a mark, each relationship an echo of her past pain. She yearned for someone who would see her beyond the surface and help her heal.

Mishack clenched and unclenched his fists, a habit born from years of suppressing anger and fear. His own childhood had been a nightmare, a reality where trust was shattered by violence. The trauma he had experienced had left him with emotional scars that were now being replayed in his abusive relationship with Charmaine.

David stared at his reflection in the bathroom mirror, the weight of his actions pressing heavily on his shoulders. His own past mistakes seemed to have caught up with him, a cycle of betrayal that he had unwittingly perpetuated. The echoes of his own insecurities reverberated through his decisions.

In this chapter, the characters' pasts were revealed in fragments, like pieces of a jigsaw puzzle that hinted at the bigger picture. Their experiences served as a lens through which their present actions and choices could be understood. The tone was one of introspection, as each character grappled with the impact of their past on their present lives, and readers were offered a glimpse into the complex web of emotions and traumas that had brought them to this point.

THE MASK WE WEAR

The city lights shimmered around Charmaine as she danced the night away, her laughter and energy infectious. Her friends admired her vivacious spirit, envying the freedom with which she seemed to live her life. Yet, beneath the surface of her carefree façade, an ocean of pain and insecurities churned.

As the music thumped in the club, Charmaine's thoughts wandered to a time before the bright lights and laughter. A time when vulnerability had been met with betrayal and trust had been shattered. It was a lesson she had learned early, one that had shaped the protective armor she now wore.

Her gaze met David's across the dance floor, a spark of recognition and shared history flashing between them. He had been one of the few who had glimpsed beyond her mask, who had seen the wounds she tried to hide. Their connection had been both a comfort and a source of turmoil, a reminder of the pain that dwelled beneath the surface.

As the night continued, Charmaine's interactions with Mishack and Peter hinted at a complex web of emotions. Mishack's gaze held a mixture of anger and protectiveness, a reflection of his own struggles and traumas. Peter's charm and genuine interest created a different dynamic, stirring emotions Charmaine had long tried to suppress.

Charmaine's relationships with the other characters were painted with layers of history and unspoken feelings. Her connection with Patience held an undercurrent of rivalry and jealousy, born from shared history and shared pain. The masks they each wore were a barrier that kept them both at arm's length.

The chapter balanced Charmaine's outward exuberance with the underlying pain she carried. The tone was a mixture of vibrancy and melancholy, as Charmaine's façade cracked to reveal the complex emotions she battled beneath. Her relationships with the other characters were established as intricate threads that would continue to unravel throughout the story, each revealing more about her journey of healing and growth.

PART 2:

THREADS OF RESILIENCE

SHATTERED ILLUSIONS

The city's skyline was painted with hues of orange and pink as Matilda sat in her elegantly decorated living room, a calculated smile on her lips. Her web of manipulation continued to extend its reach, ensnaring those around her in a tangle of deceit.

Lorraine's brows furrowed as she recalled the strange coincidence of David's sudden late-night phone calls. A gnawing feeling of suspicion had taken root in her mind, an inkling that there was more to the story than David was letting on. She resisted the urge to confront him, the fear of the truth holding her back.

Patience scrolled through messages on her phone, the sense of control she felt over David's life intoxicating. Yet, even as she reveled in her manipulation, a nagging voice in her mind questioned the morality of her actions. Doubt crept in, a hint that her pursuit of power might come at a higher cost than she was willing to pay.

Charmaine's laughter echoed through the room as she shared a drink with Mishack, the shadows of their past traumas casting a long pall over their interactions. She caught sight of Matilda from across the room, a calculating glint in her eyes that sent a shiver down Charmaine's spine. The sense of being watched only added to her unease.

Mishack, his fists clenched at his sides, watched Matilda closely as she moved through the crowd. Her presence seemed to cast a sinister shadow, a stark contrast to the carefree atmosphere of the evening. He sensed that she held more power over the situation than anyone realized.

As the characters' suspicions continued to grow, Matilda's manipulation became increasingly apparent. The tension in the room was palpable, a reflection of the tangled web she had woven. The tone was one of heightened uncertainty, as the characters grappled with their own intuition and the unsettling realization that they were mere pawns in a game they were only beginning to understand.

LORRAINE'S CROSSROADS

The early morning sunlight filtered through the curtains, casting a soft glow on Lorraine's face as she sat at the kitchen table, her thoughts a storm of conflicting emotions. The weight of the truth bore down on her, the shattered illusions of her marriage now impossible to ignore.

David's attempts at normalcy seemed like a cruel mockery in the face of his betrayal. Lorraine's heart was torn between the love she once felt and the reality of his actions. She recalled the promises they had made, the dreams they had shared, and felt a surge of anger at how easily he had cast them aside.

The idea of rebuilding her life, of finding a path forward, began to take shape in Lorraine's mind. A spark of determination ignited within her, a whisper that she could emerge from this turmoil stronger than before. She considered the friendships she had neglected, the dreams she had set aside, and the person she had lost sight of in the midst of her marriage.

As she stared out the window, Lorraine's inner turmoil was reflected in the storm clouds gathering in the distance. She realized that she stood at a crossroads — one path leading to bitterness and despair, the other to healing and empowerment. The journey ahead was uncertain, but the choice was hers to make.

Lorraine's internal struggle was marked by a mixture of pain and hope, as she grappled with the weight of her husband's betrayal and the possibility of reclaiming her own identity. The chapter introduced the theme of rebuilding and empowerment, hinting at the transformative journey that lay ahead for Lorraine. The tone was one of introspection, as Lorraine navigated the storm within her heart while contemplating the choices that would shape her future.

UNRAVELING PATIENCE

The moon cast a silvery glow over the city as Patience sat in her dimly lit apartment, her eyes fixed on the screen of her phone. The child's innocent smile stared back at her, a reminder of the leverage she held over David. Her motives were a tangle of desires – a yearning for the life she felt she deserved and a thirst for control.

Patience's thoughts drifted back to her own past, a time when she had been vulnerable and easily manipulated. The scars of betrayal had left their mark, a reminder of the fragility of trust. It was a lesson she had learned well, a lesson that had shaped her into the manipulator she had become.

As she typed out messages to David, Patience's fingers moved with practiced precision, her words calculated to elicit a response. She reveled in the power she held, the knowledge that she could shape his actions and decisions. Yet, even as she played the puppeteer, a hint of doubt gnawed at the edges of her mind.

Patience's transformation journey was beginning, marked by a growing awareness of the consequences of her actions. The web of manipulation she had woven was both a source of empowerment and a prison of her own making. The chapter delved into her motives and tactics, shedding light on the complex emotions that drove her decisions.

As the moonlight bathed her surroundings, Patience's journey of transformation was set in motion. The tone was one of intrigue and introspection, as Patience grappled with the realization that the path she had chosen might lead to an unexpected destination – one that challenged her perception of power and control.

HIDDEN SCARS

The room was dimly lit, the shadows on the walls a reflection of the memories that haunted Mishack's mind. He sat in silence; his gaze fixed on a cracked photograph that captured a fragment of his childhood. The image was a portal to a past marked by trauma and abuse, scars that had shaped the man he had become.

Mishack's thoughts drifted back to his early years, a time when innocence had been stolen from him. The faces of his parents, once sources of love and safety, were now tangled in a web of violence and fear. He had witnessed things no child should ever see, and the echoes of that darkness reverberated through his adult life.

As he navigated his relationship with Charmaine, Mishack found himself caught in a cycle of violence he had vowed to escape. The anger that simmered beneath the surface was a reminder of the past he had never fully dealt with. Each time he clenched his fists, he felt the weight of his history pressing down on him.

The complexity of Mishack's character was evident in the juxtaposition of his strength and vulnerability. The scars he carried were both visible and hidden, shaping his interactions with those around him. His protective instincts clashed with his own inner demons, leaving him torn between the desire to break free and the fear of repeating history.

In this chapter, Mishack's history of trauma and abuse was unveiled, offering insight into the complexity of his character. The tone was a blend of introspection and melancholy, as Mishack grappled with the impact of his past on his present actions. His relationship with Charmaine provided a backdrop to his internal struggle, highlighting the deep wounds that still needed healing.

FRACTURED TRUST

The city's skyline was painted with hues of twilight as the characters found themselves gathered in different corners of the same space. The air was thick with unspoken tension, the strain in their relationships palpable as the weight of deceit cast a long shadow over their interactions.

Lorraine's gaze met David's across the room, the flicker of hurt and suspicion evident in her eyes. The trust that had once been the foundation of their marriage had been shattered, and now a chasm of uncertainty yawned between them. Her heart ached with the realization that the person she had thought she knew was a stranger.

Patience exchanged fleeting glances with David, a smirk of satisfaction playing on her lips. Her manipulation was a weapon she wielded with precision, yet even as she reveled in her control, a nagging doubt crept in. The satisfaction of power was tainted by the emptiness of deceit.

Charmaine's laughter was a façade that barely masked the tension she felt. Her interactions with the men in the room held a mix of longing and bitterness, a reflection of the pain that had woven its way into her relationships. Her connection with Mishack was marked by a blend of desire and fear, a mirror of the history they both carried.

Mishack's fists clenched at his sides, his inner turmoil mirrored in the tension of his body. The violence he had witnessed as a child had left an indelible mark, and now its echoes reverberated through his relationship with Charmaine. The distance between them was a testament to the fractures that deceit had created.

As the chapter unfolded, the strain in the characters' relationships was vividly portrayed, a result of the tangled web of lies and manipulation that had woven itself around them. The tone was one of unease and impending reckoning, foreshadowing the need for healing and the difficult paths that lay ahead for each character.

PART 3:

WHISPERS OF CHANGE

A GLIMPSE OF TRUTH

The moon hung low in the night sky as the characters found themselves drawn together by an invisible force, a web of deceit that had begun to unravel. The whispers of truth lingered in the air, and as they pieced together the fragments of Matilda's manipulations, their reactions ranged from shock to confusion.

Lorraine sat at the kitchen table; the incriminating messages laid out before her. A knot tightened in her chest as the pieces fell into place, revealing the extent of David's betrayal. Her fingers trembled as she reread his messages to Patience, each word a cruel reminder of his infidelity. The walls of her reality crumbled around her, leaving her feeling adrift in a sea of uncertainty.

Patience's smirk faded as she read the message from David, his tone shifting from affection to desperation. She had reveled in her control over him, but now a creeping unease settled in. The satisfaction of manipulation was marred by the guilt of exploiting their shared past, and she questioned whether the power she wielded was worth the price of her integrity.

Charmaine's heart raced as she stumbled upon a message that hinted at the orchestrated encounters she had shared with David. The realization that Matilda had been pulling the strings behind the scenes left her feeling exposed, her sense of agency slipping through her fingers. The confusion in her eyes mirrored the turmoil within her as she grappled with the implications of the truth.

Mishack's fists clenched as he overheard snippets of conversation, the puzzle pieces falling into place in his mind. The depth of Matilda's manipulation became clear, and a storm of anger brewed within him. The history of violence he had fought to escape was now resurfacing in a new form, and the confusion he felt was underscored by a burning desire for justice.

As the characters uncovered the truth, the web of lies that Matilda had woven began to unravel. The chapter was tinged with a mix of shock, confusion, and anger, as each character grappled with the implications of the revelations. The tone was one of heightened tension and uncertainty, a prelude to the confrontations and transformations that lay ahead.

SEEKING REDEMPTION

The sun cast long shadows on the city streets as Charmaine found herself standing at a crossroads. The weight of her past choices bore down on her, a burden she could no longer ignore. A fire of determination burned within her, a flicker of hope that she could mend her ways and confront the demons that haunted her.

With each step she took, Charmaine's journey felt like a trek through a minefield of memories. The façade of confidence she had worn for so long crumbled, revealing the vulnerability that had been carefully concealed. She had danced through life, using parties and men as distractions from the pain she carried. But now, she was ready to face the truth.

As she delved into her past, Charmaine's internal struggle was a tempest of emotions. Memories of her own abuse resurfaced, a reality she had long buried beneath layers of denial. The weight of shame and guilt threatened to consume her, but she pressed on, determined to find a path to redemption.

Charmaine sought guidance in unexpected places, reaching out to support groups and mentors who could help her navigate her journey of healing. The process was agonizing, each step forward met with the resistance of old wounds. The temptation to revert to old habits was a siren's call, but she fought to silence it.

The chapter depicted Charmaine's struggle with raw vulnerability, as she confronted her past and sought redemption for the choices she had made. The tone was one of introspection and determination, as she embarked on a quest to untangle the web of pain that had held her captive for so long. Her journey was marked by setbacks and moments of triumph, offering a glimpse into the complexity of healing and growth.

PATIENCE'S AWAKENING

The moon hung low in the night sky as Patience sat alone in her apartment, the glow of her phone illuminating her contemplative expression. The messages she had exchanged with David were like a heavy weight around her neck, a reminder of the manipulation she had allowed herself to sink into.

A wave of self-awareness washed over her, a realization that her pursuit of power had come at the cost of her own integrity. The satisfaction she had once felt now seemed shallow; the emptiness of her victories more pronounced. Her motives were a jumble of desires – a yearning for control, a hunger for validation, and a thirst for something deeper.

As Patience revisited her own history, memories of her vulnerable moments resurfaced. She saw herself as a girl who had been hurt, a girl who had learned to protect herself by wielding her own brand of manipulation. The façade of strength she had constructed was now cracking, revealing the layers of insecurity beneath.

With each passing day, Patience's transformation journey gained momentum. She reached out to therapists and support groups, seeking guidance in her quest for change. The process was far from easy – she faced resistance from within herself, the allure of her old tactics often pulling her back.

Yet, even as she stumbled, Patience's determination remained unshaken. She started making amends, taking steps to mend the bridges she had burned. Her actions were cautious, each apology a thread in the tapestry of her redemption. And with each small act of vulnerability, she discovered a glimmer of the person she could become.

The chapter captured Patience's journey toward self-awareness and change, as she grappled with the consequences of her actions and sought to unearth the layers of her own motivations. The tone was one of introspection and growth, as she navigated the complexities of transformation while facing the challenges of her past.

BONDS STRENGTHENED

The city's skyline glittered under the starlit sky as the characters found themselves drawn together by a common purpose. The truth they had uncovered about Matilda's manipulation had become a rallying point, a catalyst for unity amidst the chaos that had surrounded them.

Lorraine's determination burned brightly as she met with the others in a quiet corner of a café. The pain of betrayal was still fresh, but now it was mingled with a shared resolve to confront the puppeteer who had manipulated their lives. Her eyes met those of the others, and in that moment, a silent pact was formed.

Patience's usual confidence wavered slightly as she spoke, her voice carrying the weight of her own guilt and longing for change. She revealed the extent of her manipulation and the role she had played in Matilda's game. Her admission was met with a mixture of understanding and empathy, the realization dawning that they were all victims of a larger scheme.

Charmaine's demeanor was a mixture of vulnerability and determination as she shared her struggles to break free from her past. Her journey toward redemption was met with nods of encouragement, the unspoken acknowledgment that they were all on a path of transformation. Her vulnerability was met with compassion, erasing the walls that had once divided them.

Mishack's fists were no longer clenched in anger, but rather in solidarity. He opened up about the violence he had witnessed and experienced, the trauma that had bound them all together in unexpected ways. The realization that they could support each other in healing was a beacon of hope amidst the darkness of their pasts.

As the chapter unfolded, the characters' shared determination to confront Matilda was vividly portrayed. The bond that had formed among them was a testament to their resilience and their shared quest for truth. The tone was one of unity and resolve, as they prepared to face the puppeteer who had manipulated their lives and unravel the tangled web she had woven.

CRACKS IN THE FACADE

The city's lights cast a soft glow over Matilda's elegant living room as she sat alone, a sense of unease gnawing at the edges of her composure. The mask of control she had worn for so long was beginning to crack, revealing glimpses of the vulnerabilities she had fought to hide.

As memories of her past resurfaced, Matilda's thoughts drifted to a time when she had been young and vulnerable. Her family had crumbled under the weight of their own dysfunction, leaving her with scars that had never fully healed. The lessons she had learned about power and manipulation had been forged in the crucible of her own trauma.

Matilda's gaze fell on a photograph on the mantel, a picture of a smiling family that belied the turmoil that had existed beneath the surface. The wounds of her past had shaped her into the puppeteer she had become, a master of manipulation who sought control over others as a means of protection.

As she traced her fingers over the photograph, a sense of self-awareness settled in. Matilda had built walls around herself, walls that had kept her safe but had also isolated her from genuine connections. The realization that she had become the very thing she had despised in her own upbringing was a bitter pill to swallow.

The chapter began to humanize Matilda's character, shedding light on her own trauma and history. The tone was one of vulnerability and introspection, as Matilda grappled with the cracks in her façade and the ghosts of her past. Her journey toward self-awareness was marked by a mixture of regret and the tentative beginnings of change.

PART 4:

EMBRACING LIGHT

BREAKING POINT

The room was charged with tension as the characters confronted Matilda, their shared determination palpable in the air. The truth they had uncovered had led them to this moment of reckoning, where the puppeteer would face the consequences of her manipulation.

Lorraine's voice trembled slightly as she spoke, her eyes fixed on Matilda's. She recounted the messages, the lies, and the shattered trust that had once been the cornerstone of her marriage. The pain in her words was a mirror of the pain etched on her face, a testament to the devastation Matilda's actions had wrought.

Patience's resolve was unwavering as she spoke of the manipulation she had succumbed to, the realization that she had allowed herself to become a tool of Matilda's schemes. Her voice held a mixture of regret and determination, a reflection of her journey toward changes and redemption.

Charmaine's vulnerability was a stark contrast to the bravado she had once worn like armor. She spoke of the pain she had buried beneath layers of parties and shallow connections, the trauma that had shaped her into someone she barely recognized. Her voice wavered, but her determination to heal was unshakeable.

Mishack's anger burned brightly as he confronted Matilda, his words laced with the echoes of his own past trauma. He held her accountable for the abuse he had experienced, his voice a fierce declaration of the strength he had found in facing his demons. The anger in his eyes was a mirror of the rage that had once consumed him.

As the characters' emotions spilled over, Matilda's façade began to crack further. The emotional showdown that followed was a storm of anger, pain, and vulnerability. Accusations and revelations echoed in the room, the tension escalating until it reached a breaking point.

The chapter depicted the confrontation as an emotional crescendo, a culmination of the characters' journeys and the revelation of Matilda's manipulation. The tone was one of raw intensity, as emotions boiled over and the characters confronted the puppeteer who had woven their lives into a tangled web.

HEALING HEARTS

The aftermath of the emotional showdown left the characters in a state of disarray. The revelations had shattered their perceptions and exposed the wounds they had each carried. As they grappled with the weight of the truth, the journey toward healing began, though forgiveness remained a distant horizon.

Lorraine's gaze was a mix of anger and hurt as she looked at Matilda, her voice laced with disbelief. The woman who had once been a trusted friend was now a stranger, a manipulator who had woven a web of deceit around them. The words Matilda spoke were like shards of glass, cutting into Lorraine's heart.

Patience's struggle was evident in the furrow of her brows and the clenching of her jaw. The realization that she had willingly played a part in Matilda's schemes weighed heavily on her conscience. Forgiving herself was a daunting task, and the path toward change felt like an uphill battle.

Charmaine's eyes were haunted, her vulnerability exposed to the harsh light of truth. The pain she had suppressed for so long had been laid bare, and the knowledge that she had allowed herself to be controlled stung deeply. Forgiveness seemed like an unattainable goal, and yet the seed of healing had been planted.

Mishack's anger had simmered into a complex mix of emotions – rage, sorrow, and a desire for closure. The confrontation had given him a taste of justice, but forgiveness remained elusive. The scars of his past still marked him, a reminder that healing was a process that required time and effort.

The characters' reactions to Matilda's revelations were a tapestry of emotions, each struggling to come to terms with the extent of the manipulation. The chapter delved into their internal struggles with forgiveness, capturing the complexities of letting go of anger and resentment. The tone was one of introspection and emotional turmoil, as they navigated the uncharted waters of healing.

PATH TO REDEMPTION

The city streets were washed in the soft light of dawn as Mishack stood before the mirror, his gaze fixed on his own reflection. The anger that had defined so much of his life stared back at him, a reminder of the cycle of abuse he was determined to break. The path to redemption stretched ahead, challenging him to confront his past and rewrite his future.

Mishack's days were a montage of efforts to change, a series of conscious choices to rewrite the script of his life. He sought therapy to untangle the knots of his trauma, determined to understand the roots of his anger and violence. Each session was a journey into the darkness he had long avoided, a step toward the light of healing.

His interactions with Charmaine took on a new dynamic as he learned to communicate without fists or anger. The vulnerability he allowed himself to feel was both liberating and terrifying, a departure from the patterns he had known. The desire to protect her from his own darkness fueled his determination to change.

Mishack's transformation journey was marked by setbacks and triumphs. There were moments when he stumbled, when the echoes of his past threatened to pull him back into the abyss. But he clung to the glimmers of hope he had found, the vision of a future where he could break free from the cycle of abuse.

As the chapter unfolded, Mishack's journey toward redemption was depicted with a mix of introspection and determination. The tone was one of struggle and hope, as he navigated the challenges of confronting his past and rewriting his future. His efforts to change his behavior and break free from the cycle of abuse were a testament to the power of transformation.

REBUILDING BRIDGES

The city's skyline shifted as day turned to dusk, a metaphor for the characters' own journeys from darkness to a glimmer of light. With the truth exposed and wounds bared, they now faced the formidable task of rebuilding trust and relationships that had been fractured by deception.

Lorraine's attempts to mend her marriage were met with a mix of hope and skepticism. The wounds of betrayal ran deep, and the road to rebuilding trust was marked by a series of difficult conversations and tentative steps. Forgiveness was a distant horizon, and yet the love that had once bound them was a beacon of possibility.

Patience's efforts to change her ways were met with skepticism from those around her. The lingering doubt of her motives cast a shadow over her every action, and the challenge of proving her sincerity was an uphill battle. The path to redemption was fraught with setbacks, but each small act of honesty was a brick in the bridge she was building.

Charmaine's struggle to confront her past continued as she sought to mend her relationships. The echoes of her past actions still resonated in the way others looked at her, the challenge of shedding her old identity a constant battle. Her attempts to rebuild trust were marked by vulnerability and self-doubt, the fear that she was too broken to be redeemed.

Mishack's transformation journey brought him face-to-face with the challenge of breaking the cycle of abuse. His attempts to rebuild his relationship with Charmaine were a reflection of his desire to rewrite the narrative of his past. Yet, the fear of slipping back into old habits was a constant shadow, a reminder of the darkness he had fought to escape.

The chapter depicted the characters' efforts to rebuild trust and relationships, emphasizing the challenges they faced in doing so. The tone was one of uncertainty and hope, as they navigated the intricacies of forgiveness, vulnerability, and the slow process of healing wounds that had been inflicted by their own actions and the manipulation of others.

WHISPERS OF TRANSFORMATION

The city's skyline shimmered under the setting sun, a reflection of the journeys the characters had undertaken. Their paths had been marked by pain, betrayal, and manipulation, but as they stood on the threshold of a new chapter, the whispers of transformation were unmistakable.

Lorraine's heart had been shattered, her trust in David irreparably damaged. Yet, the journey had also brought her a newfound strength – a strength born from the crucible of betrayal. She stood tall, a woman who had navigated the storm and emerged with the fragments of her identity reclaimed.

Patience's path to redemption had been fraught with challenges, but her determination to change had sparked a metamorphosis within her. The manipulation that had once defined her was now replaced by empathy and authenticity. Her journey was far from over, but the whispers of transformation hinted at a future where she could truly heal.

Charmaine's façade had crumbled, revealing the woman beneath the bravado. Her quest for redemption had been a rollercoaster of emotions, a journey through the darkest corners of her past. As she rebuilt her relationships and faced her demons, the whispers of transformation painted a picture of a future where she could finally be free.

Mishack's battle against his own past had brought him to a crossroads. The echoes of abuse had begun to fade, replaced by a newfound sense of self-worth and a determination to break the cycle. The transformation was a slow burn, but the whispers of change echoed in his every choice, a promise of a future where violence would no longer define him.

As the characters' journeys converged, the city's skyline seemed to glow with a sense of hope. The whispers of transformation were a testament to their resilience and the power of change. The future remained uncertain, but the stories etched in their hearts were a testament to the strength they had discovered within themselves.

PART 5:

RESILIENCE AWAKENED

PATHS CONVERGED

The city's heartbeat pulsed in rhythm with the characters' breaths as they stood at the crossroads of their journeys. The echoes of their individual transformations reverberated in the air; their choices now intertwined in a collective tapestry of change. Each faced pivotal decisions, their paths converging in a way that would shape their shared future.

Lorraine's gaze was steady as she looked at David, the wounds of betrayal still fresh but a glimmer of something new in her eyes. The journey she had undertaken had empowered her, and now she stood at a juncture – to forgive, to rebuild, or to walk away. Her decision held the weight of her own transformation and the potential for a future reshaped by her choices.

Patience's phone buzzed with a message from David, a reminder of the power she still held. But the satisfaction of manipulation had lost its luster, replaced by the growing awareness of the impact of her actions on others. She faced a choice – to continue down the path of control or to embrace the vulnerability of authenticity that her transformation had unveiled.

Charmaine's steps were uncertain as she approached Mishack, the echoes of her old self a distant memory. The journey of redemption had opened her eyes to the damage she had caused, and now she stood before him with a question – to rebuild what they had or to forge a new connection based on their shared growth. Her decision would define the future they could create together.

Mishack's fists were no longer clenched, his transformation evident in his demeanor. The violence of his past had given way to a newfound strength rooted in healing and self-discovery. The choice before him was whether to hold onto the remnants of anger or to let go, embracing the whispers of transformation that had guided him toward a better path.

As the characters' paths converged, the chapter depicted their individual transformations impacting their collective journey. The tone was one of contemplation and anticipation, as each character grappled with the choices before them. The crossroads they faced were not only a culmination of their personal growth but also a testament to the way their stories had become intertwined.

THREADS OF CONNECTION

The city's hustle and bustle faded into the background as the characters found themselves drawn together by an invisible thread of connection. The shared experiences, pain, and growth they had undergone had woven bonds that transcended the superficial. In the midst of their own individual transformations, they discovered the power of unity and support.

Lorraine's voice trembled as she shared her doubts and fears with Patience, the woman who had once been a source of resentment now a pillar of empathy. Their conversations were marked by vulnerability, a testament to the healing that could be found in shared experiences. Their connection was a lifeline, a reminder that they were not alone in their struggles.

Patience's journey toward change had been a solitary one, but now she found herself leaning on Charmaine for guidance and understanding. The woman she had once seen as an adversary had become an ally, their shared experiences creating a bridge of empathy. Through late-night conversations and tears shed in the darkness, their bond grew stronger.

Charmaine's transformation journey had been one of shedding the layers of her old self, and now she found solace in Mishack's presence. Their shared struggles and the battles they had fought within themselves created a silent understanding. Their connection was a reminder that even the most broken pieces could come together to form something beautiful.

Mishack's steps toward change had led him to a place of newfound strength, and his support for Lorraine was unwavering. The history of violence that had once defined him had been replaced by a commitment to protect and uplift. His bond with Lorraine was a testament to the power of growth, a reminder that the threads of connection could mend even the deepest wounds.

As the chapter unfolded, the deepening bonds between the characters were depicted with a mix of intimacy and authenticity. The power of shared experiences and growth was evident in their interactions, as they leaned on each other for support and understanding. The tone was one of warmth and camaraderie, illustrating the way their collective journey had reshaped their connections.

REFLECTIONS IN THE MIRROR

The city's lights shimmered in the night as the characters found themselves engaged in moments of quiet introspection. The whirlwind of their transformations had brought them to this point, where they stood at the precipice of change, looking within themselves to evaluate their progress and setbacks.

Lorraine's reflection stared back at her in the mirror, the woman she had become a far cry from the one who had once defined herself solely through her marriage. The journey of self-discovery had been marked by highs and lows, moments of strength and moments of doubt. She recognized that true transformation came from within, a journey she was still navigating.

Patience's gaze lingered on her own reflection, the woman who had once reveled in manipulation now seeking authenticity. The setbacks she had encountered were reminders of the long road ahead, but they were also testaments to her resilience. She had learned that the path to change was paved with self-awareness and the courage to confront one's own flaws.

Charmaine's eyes held a mixture of determination and vulnerability as she looked at herself, the woman who had once used parties as a shield against pain. The progress she had made was undeniable, but the journey had been far from linear. She understood that true transformation required confronting the shadows within oneself, a process that could not be rushed.

Mishack's reflection was that of a man who had battled his own demons and emerged stronger. The violence of his past was no longer the defining factor of his identity. He had realized that the path to change was an internal one – a journey toward self-love and self-forgiveness. The setbacks were part of the process, reminders that growth required patience.

RECKONING WITH SHADOWS

The city's skyline was a backdrop to the storm of emotions that raged within Matilda as she stood before the characters she had manipulated. The consequences of her actions had caught up with her, and now she faced a reckoning – not just from those she had harmed, but from the person she had become.

Lorraine's voice was firm, her gaze unwavering as she held Matilda accountable for the pain she had caused. The betrayal of a trusted friend had left scars that were slow to heal, and now the puppeteer was stripped of her power, laid bare in the face of the truth. Matilda's internal struggle was evident in the clenching of her fists, the battle of pride against guilt.

Patience's voice trembled with a mix of anger and sorrow as she confronted the woman who had manipulated her own desires. The manipulation had revealed her own flaws and the harm she had inflicted on others. Matilda's internal turmoil mirrored her own as she faced the mirror of her past choices, the shadows of her actions cast into stark relief.

Charmaine's voice, once filled with bravado, was now laced with vulnerability as she looked at Matilda. The woman who had once controlled her was now confronted by her own demons. Matilda's struggle was a reflection of the internal battles that Charmaine herself had fought, a reminder that the facade of strength could be shattered by the weight of truth.

Mishack's anger was palpable as he addressed Matilda, the echoes of his own past pain driving his words. He held her accountable for the violence she had orchestrated, a violence that had haunted him for years. Matilda's internal struggle was a mirror of his own as she faced the consequences of her actions, the shadows of her past choices casting a long shadow over her.

ECHOES OF FORGIVENESS

The city's lights flickered in the night as the characters found themselves grappling with the concept of forgiveness. The echoes of their past pain and the transformations they had undergone had led them to this moment, where the weight of grudges hung heavy in the air, juxtaposed against the possibility of releasing them.

Lorraine's thoughts were a mixture of anger and a yearning for closure as she considered forgiving David. The wounds of his betrayal still smarted, but the journey of self-discovery had opened a door to the possibility of healing. Her internal struggle was a reflection of the complex emotions that forgiveness stirred – the desire to let go warring with the pain of the past.

Patience's internal battle was etched on her face as she contemplated the idea of forgiving Matilda. The manipulation that had once bound them now seemed like chains she wanted to break free from. Yet, the journey of her own transformation had taught her that forgiveness wasn't just about absolving others – it was also about freeing herself from the grip of resentment.

Charmaine's thoughts were a whirlwind of conflicting emotions as she looked at Mishack. The violence he had once perpetrated against her had scarred her deeply, and yet the changes he had undergone were evident. Forgiveness felt like a fragile thread, a choice to release the grip of anger that had defined her for so long.

Mishack's gaze was steady as he faced Charmaine, the shadows of his past pain etched in his eyes. He understood the weight of his actions and the difficulty of forgiveness. The internal struggle he experienced was a mirror of the emotions that Charmaine grappled with – the desire to be free from anger warring against the memories of the pain inflicted.

PART 6

RISING FROM THE ASHES

SEEDS OF CHANGE

The city's streets were cloaked in darkness as Matilda found herself alone in her lavish apartment, memories of her past haunting her thoughts. The time had come to delve deeper into the shadows of her history, to uncover the seeds of pain that had driven her to manipulation and control. As the characters began to understand her background, their perceptions shifted in unexpected ways.

Matilda's thoughts drifted back to her childhood, to the fractured family that had left scars that ran deep. The echoes of dysfunction, abuse, and betrayal had become the foundation upon which she had built her walls. The manipulation that had once been her defense mechanism had been born from the need to protect herself from further pain.

As the characters began to uncover the pieces of Matilda's past, their perceptions of her shifted. The woman who had once been a puppeteer now appeared as a survivor, a victim of her own trauma. Understanding the roots of her actions illuminated the complexity of her motivations, forcing them to grapple with the gray areas of right and wrong.

Lorraine's anger began to shift to empathy as she learned about Matilda's past. The pain she had caused was undeniable, but the realization that she had also suffered shaped a new layer of understanding. The journey of forgiveness felt less impossible as Lorraine saw the layers of pain that had shaped the woman before her.

Patience's judgment began to waver as she heard about Matilda's upbringing. The manipulation that had once felt like a calculated attack now seemed like a desperate attempt to regain control. Patience's own journey of transformation allowed her to recognize the shared pain that had driven them both.

Charmaine's perception of Matilda was also reshaped by the revelation of her past. The woman who had once seemed like an enemy now appeared as a reflection of her own struggles. Charmaine's path toward redemption allowed her to see the potential for change even in the most broken of individuals.

Mishack's anger began to mix with a somber understanding as he listened to Matilda's story. The violence that had once defined him had roots in his own trauma, and the realization that they were both products of pain created an unexpected connection. The seeds of change had been sown, and the possibility of transformation was extended even to Matilda.

EMBRACING HOPE

The city's skyline shimmered in the early morning light, a reflection of the characters' newfound sense of possibility. As they stood on the cusp of change, the pain of their histories began to fade into the background, replaced by the spark of hope for a brighter future.

Lorraine's thoughts were a mixture of trepidation and excitement as she considered the path ahead. The pain of David's betrayal still lingered, but the journey of self-discovery had shown her that her worth was not defined by her marriage. The spark of hope ignited within her, a determination to carve out a future that was free from the shadows of her past.

Patience's steps were more confident now, her journey of transformation a roadmap to a new life. The manipulation that had once defined her was becoming a distant memory, replaced by the whispers of authenticity and growth. The determination to embrace hope was a guiding force, a reminder that she had the power to shape her own narrative.

Charmaine's heart felt lighter as she looked at Mishack, the weight of her past slowly lifting. The journey of redemption had brought her to a place where the pain of her actions was no longer a defining factor. The vision of a future free from manipulation and regret fueled her determination to embrace hope, to believe that change was possible.

Mishack's strides were filled with purpose as he walked alongside Charmaine, the echoes of his past pain fading into the distance. The transformation he had undergone was a testament to the power of change, and the hope for a life free from violence was a beacon guiding his steps. The determination to leave his painful history behind was unwavering.

As the chapter unfolded, the characters' journey of embracing hope was depicted with a mix of optimism and determination. The tone was one of renewal and anticipation, as they looked forward to a future that was defined by growth and healing. The pain of their pasts was still present, but it was no longer the driving force in their lives – instead, hope took its place, lighting the way to a brighter tomorrow.

LIBERATION UNVEILED

The city's lights danced on the horizon as Matilda found herself alone in her opulent apartment, the weight of her actions pressing down on her. The time had come to confront her own demons, to free herself from the cycle of manipulation that had defined her for so long. As she embarked on a journey of redemption, the echoes of her transformation and self-discovery began to reverberate.

Matilda's journey of self-discovery led her down a path of introspection, where she confronted the pain that had driven her to manipulate and control. The scars of her past, the fractures within her family, and the betrayal she had experienced had woven a complex tapestry of emotions. The liberation she sought was not just from the consequences of her actions, but from the internal turmoil that had held her captive.

With each step, Matilda faced the shadows of her past, acknowledging her flaws and the harm she had inflicted on others. The facade of control began to crumble, revealing a woman who was just as wounded as those she had manipulated. The journey towards redemption was marked by humility, a willingness to confront her own darkness and strive for change.

As Matilda's journey unfolded, the characters around her began to witness her transformation. The woman who had once been a puppeteer was now stripped of her manipulation, standing before them as a vulnerable human being. Their perceptions of her shifted once again, this time towards a begrudging empathy and a cautious hope for her redemption.

Lorraine's gaze softened as she observed Matilda's struggle, recognizing the familiar pain of confronting one's past. The journey of self-discovery was a difficult one, and Lorraine's empathy extended to the woman who had once been her friend. The hope for Matilda's redemption was a reflection of her own transformation – a belief that people could change.

Patience's skepticism wavered as she saw Matilda's attempts to free herself from manipulation. The journey of transformation they had both undergone created a bond, an understanding of the uphill battle she faced. Patience's own path towards change had taught her that redemption was possible, and she held onto that hope for Matilda as well.

Charmaine's eyes held a mixture of surprise and curiosity as she witnessed Matilda's internal struggle. The woman who had once held power over her was now fighting her own battles. Charmaine's journey of redemption had taught her that change was a process, and she recognized the effort it took to break free from old patterns.

Mishack's steps were steady as he approached Matilda, the shadows of his past pain reflected in his gaze. The violence he had once inflicted upon her was a testament to the cycle of abuse they had both been trapped in. Mishack's journey towards transformation had shown him the power of change, and he hoped that Matilda could find her own liberation.

The chapter depicted Matilda's journey towards redemption and self-discovery, illustrating her attempts to free herself from manipulation and confront her own demons. The tone was one of introspection and vulnerability, as she navigated the difficult path of change. The echoes of her transformation impacted not only her own perceptions but also the way those around her began to view her journey.

THREADS INTERTWINED

The city's skyline stretched out in a tapestry of lights, mirroring the threads of connection that had woven the characters' lives together. Their journeys of transformation, pain, and growth had created a complex web of shared experiences, intertwining their stories in ways they could never have imagined.

Lorraine's heart felt lighter as she looked at the people who had become her pillars of support. The pain of betrayal had been transformed into a testament of her own strength, and the friendships she had forged were a reminder that she was not alone. The threads of connection had become lifelines, binding them together in a tapestry of resilience.

Patience's steps were more confident now as she navigated her new life, the journey of transformation impacting not only herself but those around her. The threads of connection she had formed were a reminder of the power of authenticity, a bond that had been woven through shared struggles and the desire for change.

Charmaine's smile was genuine as she looked at the people who had seen her at her worst and embraced her as she worked towards her best. The journey of redemption had not only changed her own life but had also created a ripple effect that touched those around her. The threads of connection were a testament to the way shared experiences could change lives.

Mishack's gaze held a mix of gratitude and determination as he surveyed the group. The violence of his past was no longer his defining feature, replaced by the connections he had formed and the growth he had undergone. The threads of connection were a reflection of the way shared pain could lead to shared healing, a bond that transcended the pain of their histories.

As the chapter unfolded, the characters' intertwined lives were depicted with a mix of warmth and depth. The tone was one of unity and reflection, as they recognized the profound impact they had on one another. The threads of connection were a reminder that their journeys, though unique, had led them to a place of shared understanding and growth, creating a tapestry of transformation that was greater than the sum of its parts.

WHISPERS OF NEW BEGINNINGS

The city's lights glowed softly, a backdrop to the final chapter of the characters' intertwined journey. The echoes of their past pain and the threads of connection they had forged culminated in this moment – a moment of embracing their newfound strength and growth, and looking towards the future with optimism.

Lorraine stood tall; her gaze steady as she looked at the city that had witnessed her transformation. The pain of betrayal had given way to a sense of empowerment, and she had emerged from the darkness stronger than she could have ever imagined. The whispers of new beginnings were a promise that her future was hers to shape.

Patience's smile was radiant as she thought about the woman she had become. The journey of change had been difficult, but it had also been transformative. The manipulation that had once defined her was no longer a part of her identity. The whispers of new beginnings were a reminder that her story was not over – it was just beginning.

Charmaine's laughter echoed in the night air, a testament to the healing that had taken place within her. The journey of redemption had reshaped her relationships and her perception of herself. The whispers of new beginnings were a melody of hope, a promise that the future held the potential for happiness and growth.

Mishack's gaze held a quiet determination, the echoes of his past pain fading in the light of his transformation. The violence that had once defined him had been replaced by a commitment to change. The whispers of new beginnings were a reminder that the cycle of abuse had been broken, and a brighter path lay ahead.

As the characters looked at each other, the tapestry of their intertwined lives was a testament to the power of transformation. The pain of their histories had given birth to strength, resilience, and a shared bond. The whispers of new beginnings were a promise that the future was a canvas waiting to be painted with the colors of growth and healing.

The story concluded with a sense of optimism, the characters standing on the precipice of their own new beginnings. The tone was one of hope and closure, as they embraced the transformation they had undergone and looked towards the future with belief in the power of change.

PART 7:

EMBRACING THE FUTURE

DAWN OF CHANGE

The city's skyline greeted the characters with the first light of a new day, a metaphor for the dawn of change that had arrived in their lives. As they stood at the precipice of the future, they took a moment to reflect on the journey they had undertaken and the transformations they had undergone, each step shaping them into the individuals they had become.

Lorraine's thoughts were a mixture of gratitude and introspection as she gazed at the horizon. The pain of her past had been a crucible for her transformation, and the strength she had discovered within herself was a beacon of hope. As she looked towards the unknown future, the anticipation and anxiety mingled, a reminder of the uncertainty that change often brought.

Patience's eyes held a sense of wonder as she considered the distance she had traveled. The journey of change had been a rollercoaster, with unexpected twists and turns. The person she had once been felt like a distant memory, replaced by someone who had embraced growth and authenticity. The anticipation of what lay ahead was tempered by the memories of the past.

Charmaine's laughter danced in the air as she thought about the woman she had become. The journey of redemption had been a metamorphosis, and the butterfly that had emerged was a symbol of her transformation. The future held endless possibilities, but also the weight of responsibility. The anxiety of the unknown was accompanied by the excitement of shaping her destiny.

Mishack's steps were purposeful as he looked at the city he had once seen through a lens of pain. The journey of change had been a battleground, and the scars he bore were a testament to the battles he had won. The dawn of change brought with it a mix of anticipation and apprehension – the promise of a new life intermingled with the fear of slipping back into old patterns.

As the chapter unfolded, the characters' reflections on their journey and the transformations they had undergone were depicted with a mix of introspection and vulnerability. The tone was one of both excitement and anxiety, as they looked towards the horizon with a blend of hope and trepidation. The dawn of change marked not only a new chapter in their lives, but also a reminder that transformation was an ongoing process, with each day offering the potential for growth.

THREADS OF UNITY

The city's lights shimmered like stars in the night sky, mirroring the connections that had formed among the characters. Once divided by secrets, pain, and manipulation, they had now become a tightly-knit community bound by shared healing and growth. The threads of unity that had woven their lives together were a testament to the strength that could be found in collective transformation.

Lorraine's heart swelled with gratitude as she looked around at the faces that had become her chosen family. The walls that had once separated them had crumbled, replaced by a bond that was forged through shared pain and the journey of transformation. The threads of unity that connected them were a reminder that healing was a collective endeavor, and their strength lay in their unity.

Patience's smile was genuine as she exchanged knowing glances with her friends. The manipulation that had once kept them apart was now a distant memory, replaced by the understanding that they were all works in progress. The threads of unity had become a lifeline, a source of support that lifted them up when their individual journeys became overwhelming.

Charmaine's laughter filled the air, a joyful symphony that echoed the healing that had taken place within her. The threads of unity had become a safety net, a reminder that she was not alone in her battles.

The relationships she had formed were a testament to the power of vulnerability and shared growth.

Mishack's steps were steady as he walked beside his newfound friends, the echoes of his past pain fading in the presence of unity. The violence that had once isolated him was now replaced by the threads that connected them all. The threads of unity were a testament to the fact that they were stronger together – a support system that could weather any storm.

As the chapter unfolded, the characters' unity and the strength that came from shared healing were depicted with a mix of warmth and depth. The tone was one of camaraderie and empowerment, as they recognized the profound impact they had on one another's lives. The threads of unity that had once seemed fragile had become a tapestry of resilience, a reminder that the journey of transformation was one that was best traveled together.

STEPPING INTO LIGHT

The city's streets bustled with life as the characters found themselves at the crossroads of their new beginnings. The echoes of their past pain and the threads of unity that bound them gave them the courage to take bold steps forward. As they ventured into uncharted territory, they faced challenges that tested their resolve, all while striving to stay true to the growth they had achieved.

Lorraine's steps were purposeful as she embraced her new life, determined to rebuild on her own terms. The challenges she encountered were a reminder that change wasn't always smooth, but her newfound strength propelled her forward. Staying true to her growth meant facing the obstacles head-on, even when doubt and uncertainty loomed.

Patience's heart raced as she confronted the unknown, the journey of transformation an ongoing process. The challenges she faced were a reminder that old habits die hard, but her commitment to change burned bright. Staying true to her growth meant acknowledging setbacks while refusing to let them define her journey.

Charmaine's laughter mingled with the sounds of the city, a testament to her resilience in the face of challenges. The path of redemption was lined with hurdles, but her determination to stay true to her growth remained unshaken. The challenges she encountered were opportunities to demonstrate how far she had come.

Mishack's gaze was steady as he navigated the streets that once held painful memories. The challenges he faced were a reminder that transformation wasn't an instant solution, but a journey of consistent effort. Staying true to his growth meant confronting his past while also forging a future that was free from violence.

As the chapter unfolded, the characters' bold steps towards their new beginnings were depicted with a mix of determination and vulnerability. The tone was one of resilience and empowerment, as they faced the challenges that arose while holding onto the growth they had achieved. The path ahead was illuminated by the light of their transformations, a beacon that guided them even in the face of adversity.

ECHOES OF RESILIENCE

The city's streets buzzed with the rhythm of life, a backdrop to the characters' reflections on the journey that had led them to this point. The central themes of the book – trauma, resilience, and personal evolution – echoed in their thoughts, a testament to the transformative power of their experiences.

Lorraine's gaze was thoughtful as she looked at her friends, each one a living embodiment of resilience. The trauma they had endured had been the catalyst for their growth, and the challenges they had faced had only made them stronger. The echoes of resilience were a reminder that wounds could heal and that the human spirit was capable of remarkable transformation.

Patience's heart swelled with a mixture of gratitude and understanding as she thought about the shared journey of evolution they had embarked upon. The people she had once judged were now her allies in growth, a testament to the depth of human complexity. The echoes of resilience were a reminder that compassion and empathy could be found even in the most unexpected places.

Charmaine's laughter was a celebration of the strength that had emerged from the ashes of her past mistakes. The evolution she had undergone had reshaped her relationships and her perception of herself. The echoes of resilience were a chorus of redemption, a melody that illustrated the potential for change even in the face of darkness.

Mishack's steps were steady as he considered the transformation he had undergone. The violence that had once defined him had been replaced by resilience, a commitment to breaking the cycle of abuse. The echoes of resilience were a testament to the power of change, a reminder that personal evolution was not only possible but essential for healing.

As the chapter unfolded, the characters' reflections on the central themes of the book – trauma, resilience, and personal evolution – were depicted with a mix of introspection and wisdom. The tone was one of empowerment and growth, as they recognized the profound impact their journey had on their understanding of themselves and others. The echoes of resilience were a melody that played in harmony with the city's rhythm, a testament to the strength that could be found in the midst of adversity.

BREAKING DAWN

The first light of dawn painted the city in hues of gold and pink, a reflection of the closure and hope that filled the characters' hearts. The echoes of their past pain had given way to the whispers of growth and transformation, and as they stood at the threshold of a new day, they felt a sense of completion and renewal.

Lorraine's smile held a mixture of contentment and anticipation as she looked towards the horizon. The journey she had undertaken had led her to a place of healing and empowerment, but she knew that the path of growth was an ongoing one. The breaking dawn was a metaphor for the continuation of her transformation, a reminder that each day held the potential for renewal.

Patience's steps were more assured now, a reflection of the self-awareness she had gained through her journey. The breaking dawn marked a new beginning, a chance to rewrite her narrative and shape her future. The challenges that lay ahead were not daunting, but rather opportunities to put her growth into practice.

Charmaine's laughter echoed through the air, a testament to the joy she had found in her redemption. The breaking dawn symbolized a fresh start, a canvas waiting to be painted with the colors of authenticity and change. The journey she had undertaken was not without its struggles, but she had come to realize that the process of transformation was a continuous one.

Mishack's gaze held a quiet determination as he faced the breaking dawn. The violence that had once defined him was now a distant memory, replaced by a commitment to growth and healing. The breaking dawn was a metaphor for the breaking of old patterns, a reminder that he had the power to shape his own destiny.

As the chapter unfolded, the story concluded with a sense of closure and hope. The tone was one of optimism and renewal, as the characters looked towards the breaking dawn with a belief in the potential for transformation. The ending left both the characters and readers with the understanding that personal evolution was a journey that extended far beyond the pages of their story – a journey that held the promise of growth, change, and the ongoing pursuit of a better self.

EPILOGUE: WHISPERS OF TOMORROW

Time had passed since the characters had embarked on their journey of transformation, and the city's skyline remained a silent witness to the echoes of change that had reshaped their lives. The sun dipped below the horizon, casting a warm glow that illuminated the paths they had chosen, the people they had become, and the futures that lay ahead.

Lorraine's steps were confident as she navigated her bustling bakery, a testament to the business she had built from scratch. Her relationship with David had become a memory of the past, replaced by a newfound sense of independence and fulfillment. The whispers of tomorrow were a symphony of resilience, a reminder that she was the author of her own narrative.

Patience's smile was genuine as she watched her daughter play in the park, the child a testament to the change she had embraced. Her relationship with David had transformed into a co-parenting dynamic built on communication and respect. The whispers of tomorrow were a melody of growth, a reminder that the pain of the past could give birth to a future of love and possibility.

Charmaine's laughter echoed through the air as she celebrated her latest art exhibition, a reflection of the purpose she had found in her creativity. Her relationships with Mishack and the others had deepened, a testament to the power of forgiveness and second chances. The whispers of tomorrow were a chorus of redemption, a reminder that every person had the potential for change.

Mishack's gaze held a sense of peace as he stood in his art studio, the canvas before him a representation of his own evolution. The violence that had once defined him was no longer a part of his identity. His relationship with Charmaine had transformed into a partnership built on trust and mutual growth. The whispers of tomorrow were a promise of healing, a reminder that the scars of the past could become a canvas for a brighter future.

As the epilogue unfolded, a glimpse into the characters' lives sometime after the events of the book was depicted with a mix of warmth and depth. The tone was one of closure and hope, as they lived out the lasting impact of their transformations on their futures. The whispers of tomorrow were a reminder that personal growth was a journey without an end – a journey that continued to shape their lives and pave the way for a future defined by healing, authenticity, and the power of change.

~~~~~~~~~~~~~~~~~~~~~~~**END**~~~~~~~~~~~~~~~~~~~~~~~
~~~~~~~~~~~~~~~~~~~~~~~